To Abbie - J T

LITTLE TIGER PRESS

1 The Coda Centre, 189 Munster Road, London SW6 6AW
www.littletiger.co.uk

First published in Great Britain 2015

Text and illustrations copyright © Jack Tickle 2015
Visit Jack Tickle at www.ChapmanandWarnes.com
Jack Tickle has asserted his right to be identified as the author and
illustrator of this work under the Copyright, Designs and Patents Act, 1988

A CIP catalogue record for this book is available from the British Library

Printed in China • LTP/1800/1144/0415

2 4 6 8 10 9 7 5 3 1

Fish on a Dish!

Jack Tickle

Pip and Pickle are peckish.
Percy wants his dinner!

So Pickle and Pip dive in.

Splash! Whoosh! Swish!
They chase that fish.

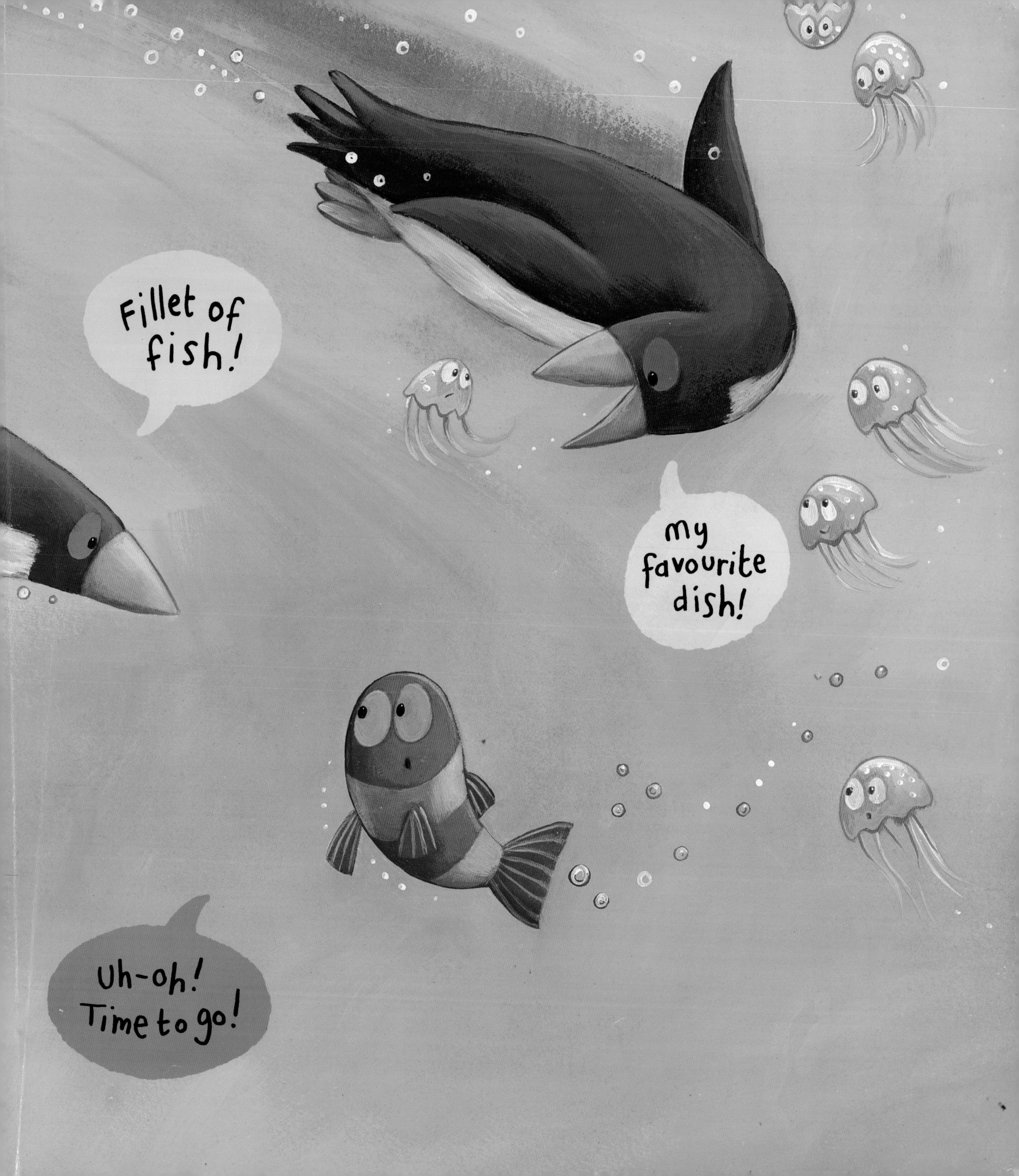
Fillet of fish!
my favourite dish!
Uh-oh! Time to go!

"He's hiding!" whispers Pip.
"But I'm HUNGRY!" moans Pickle.
Where could that little fish be?

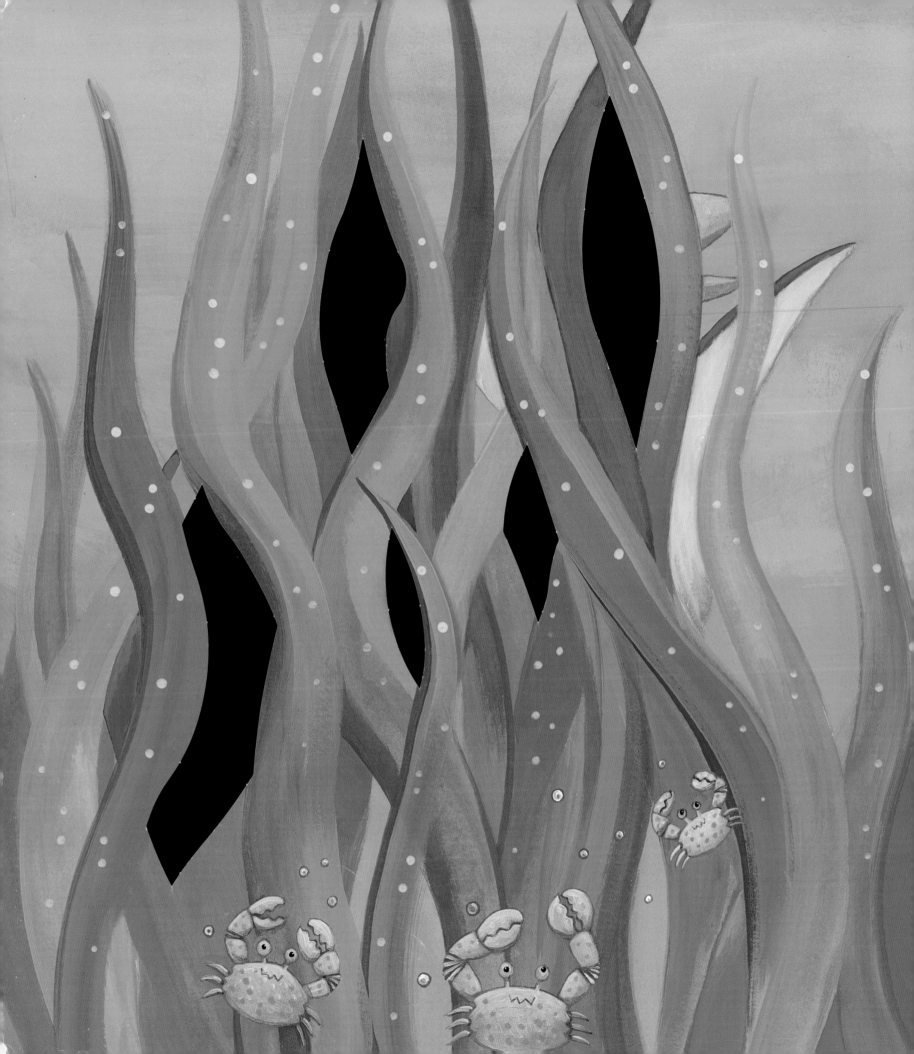

"Help!" cry the fish. "We need a plan!"

Where shall we hide?

Quick! Come inside!

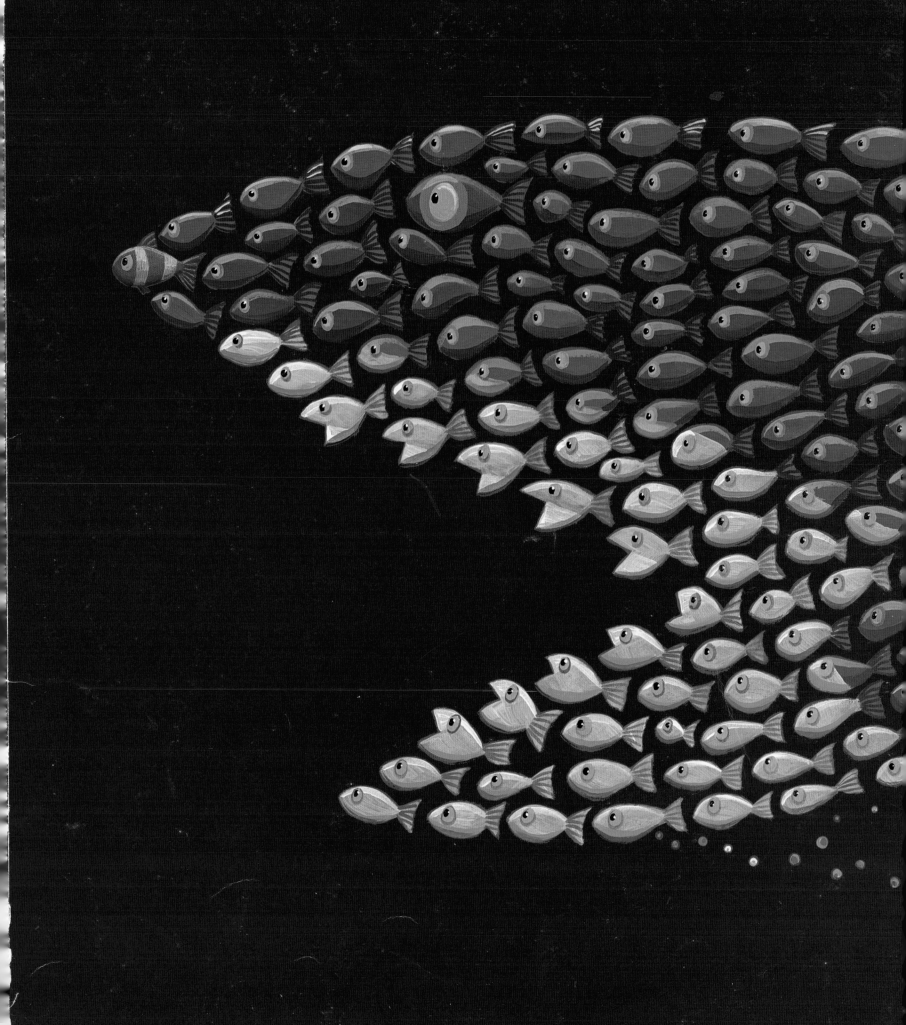

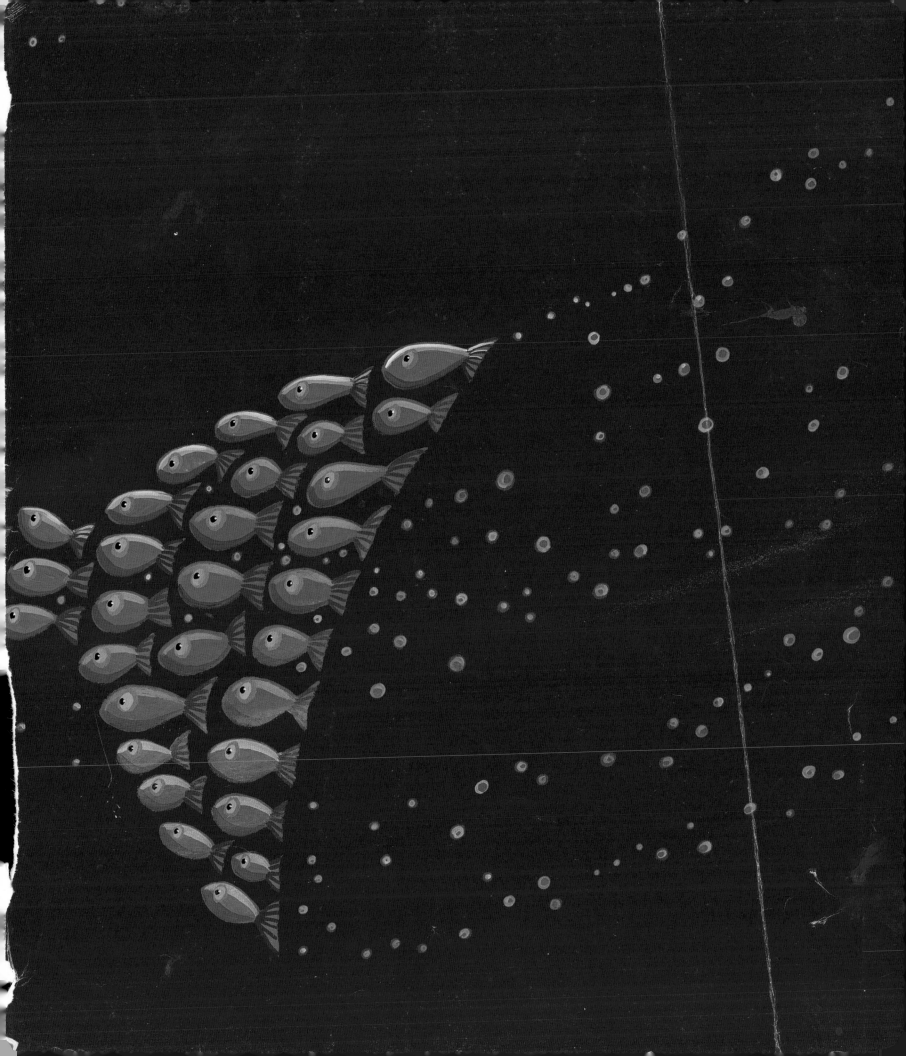

Splash! Whoosh! Swish!
Forget that fish!

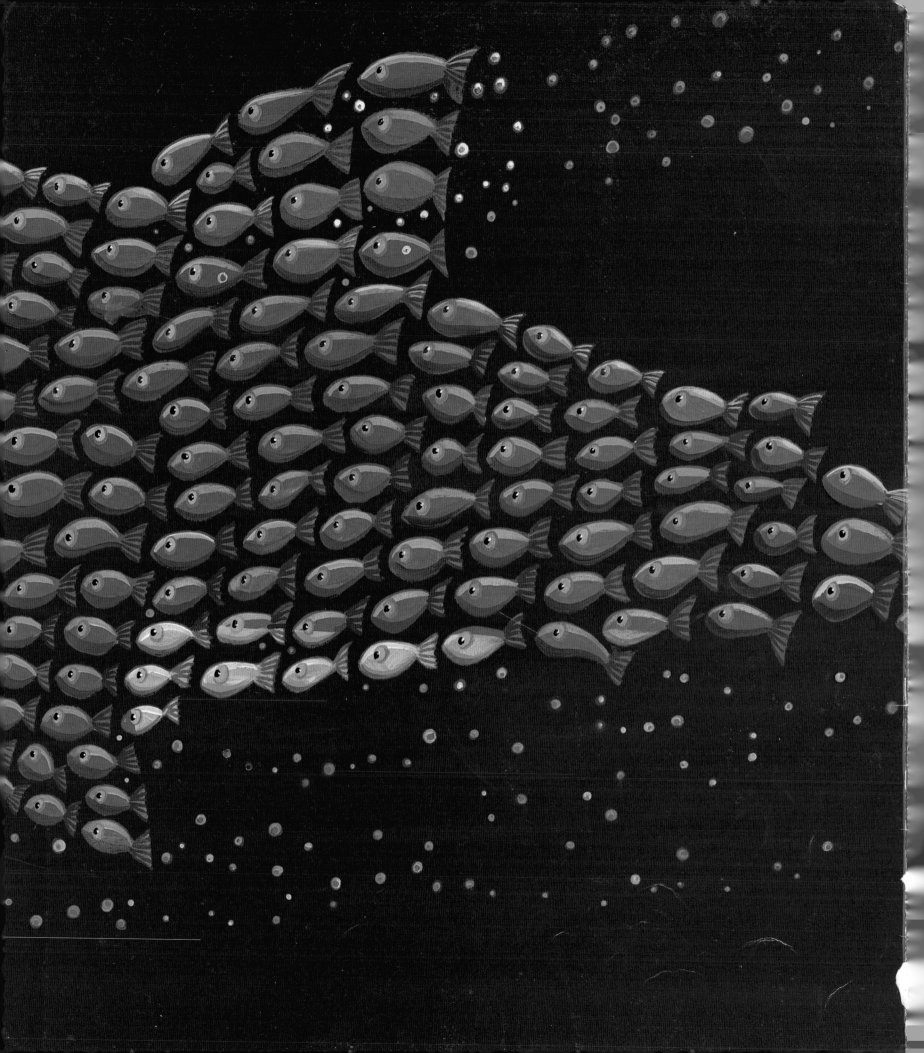

"Bother!" grumbles Percy.
"Looks like seaweed for supper AGAIN!"

Dive into another fantastic book by Jack Tickle!

Silly Dizzy Dinosaur!

Jack Tickle

For information regarding the above title or for our catalogue, please contact us:
Little Tiger Press, 1 The Coda Centre, 189 Munster Road, London SW6 6AW
Tel: 020 7385 6333 • Fax: 020 7385 7333 • E-mail: contact@littletiger.co.uk • www.littletiger.co.uk